PEANUT and the BIG FEELINGS

A GUIDEBOOK FOR CHILDREN

WRITTEN AND ILLUSTRATED BY
JENIFER TRIVELLI, M.S.

dedicated to my Peanut, my Bug,

and all the BIG feelings in the world.

ISBN: 1522799745
ISBN-13: 978-1522799740
Library of Congress Control Number: 2015921249
CreateSpace Independent Publishing Platform, North Charleston, SC

Peanut is a kid with really **BIG** feelings.

Sometimes, Peanut's feelings are **SO BIG** they **EXPLODE!**
And then legs want to run or hands want to hurt something or someone.

And sometimes, Peanut's feelings get **SO BIG** that they can't go anywhere, so they get buried down deep inside. Where they can't hurt anyone else. Where they can stay safe. And this feels very, very sad. Sometimes, it hurts so much, that Peanut doesn't want to be Peanut anymore.

One autumn day, Peanut was playing outside. Suddenly, a rustling sound came from a branch high up in the tree. Peering up at the lowest branch, Peanut made out the shape of a small, feathered friend.

It was Wise Owl.

"I've seen how sad your heart feels and how **BIG** your feelings get." said Wise Owl. "I want you to know something very important. You have a special gift, Peanut."

"I do?" Peanut asked with wide eyes.

"Yes," said Wise Owl. "Your feelings are **SO BIG** because your heart is **SO BIG**. You have an important job to do in the world and must learn how to use your **BIG** feelings to guide your **BIG** heart. I can teach you about your feelings so you will be ready to do your important job when the time comes."

Peanut's heart considered what Wise Owl said. The **BIG** feelings inside **SPARKED** and **SPARKLED**. Peanut was ready to make a change. It was time to start training with Wise Owl.

WISE OWL LESSONS

1. YOUR BODY GIVES YOU IMPORTANT CLUES.

2. YOUR WISE MIND DOESN'T WORK VERY WELL WHILE YOU'RE HAVING BIG FEELINGS BECAUSE YOUR PROTECTOR BRAIN TAKES ALL YOUR BRAIN POWER.

3. YOU CAN HELP YOUR WISE MIND WORK BY NOTICING WHAT'S AROUND YOU.

4. YOU CAN HELP YOUR WISE MIND WORK BY PAYING ATTENTION TO THE CLUES YOUR BODY GIVES YOU.

Wise Owl traced a line around Peanut's body on a l-o-o-o-o-ng piece of paper. Peanut hopped up and peered down at the outline.

"Think of a time you had a really **BIG** feeling," Wise Owl directed.

Eyes closed, Peanut remembered when a friend at school took a book away.

"Draw how that feeling felt on the paper. You can use any colors or materials you want and make it look however you want."

Wise Owl watched from the tree as Peanut picked up a marker and began.

SOME CLUES YOUR BODY GIVES YOU

bumpy

freezing

sharp

rumbling

cold

exploding

fuzzy

gurgling

hot

heavy

warm

light

bubbly

numb

scratchy

tingly

"How about your heart?" Wise Owl asked. "What was happening there?

"And your belly? Was it hot or cold? Prickly, bubbly, or still? Light or heavy?"

Peanut worked hard on the body map until it felt complete. "Wow," Peanut said. "I had no idea how much I can actually feel my feelings in my body!"

WHAT DO YOU NOTICE IN YOUR HEART RIGHT NOW? AND YOUR BELLY?

For the second lesson, Wise Owl showed Peanut a drawing of the human brain.

"The blue part, your Wise Mind, helps you make decisions that are good for you and for others. It helps you be a caring friend and take care of the planet."

"The red part, your **Protector Brain**, keeps you safe – whether that's from something hurting your body or from your feelings getting hurt. It works really *fast* – before you have a chance to stop and think."

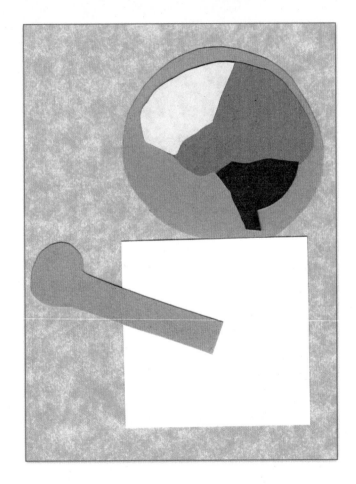

"When you get a really **BIG** feeling, your body sends your Protector Brain signals that there is **DANGER!**

"It takes all the brain power you have so it can protect you. It can't turn itself off, but it does listen to signals from your body. You need special tools to help your body signal your **Protector Brain** that it is safe. Then you can use your **Wise Mind** to make clear decisions."

Peanut thought for a minute. "When I got a really **BIG** feeling from my friend taking my book, my **BIG** feelings told my **Protector Brain** there was danger. My **Wise Mind** couldn't help me think of ways to get my book back. I just got really mad and yelled."

TELL A FRIEND OR DRAW ABOUT A TIME YOU HAD A REALLY BIG FEELING.

LESSON 3: YOU CAN HELP YOUR WISE MIND WORK BY NOTICING WHAT'S AROUND YOU

The time for the next lesson came sooner than either Peanut or Wise Owl would have guessed. Mamma called, "Peanut! Time to stop playing. Come eat dinner."

"I want to play longer Mamma."

"There's no more time for playing. I want you to come in **now.**"

Peanut recognized that tone of voice and thought, *I don't want to get ready for dinner. Mamma won't let me keep playing; she doesn't* ever *understand me or listen to me!* Peanut's **Protector Brain** started taking over brain power. Wise Owl could see Peanut's face get red. Hands balled up into fists.

"**Peanut.**" Wise Owl's voice was **strong** and **bold.** Peanut looked at Wise Owl. "I want you to let your eyes notice what's around you. Let your head and neck turn to look up, down, and side to side."

Peanut trusted Wise Owl, and even though the feelings were **BIG**, and legs wanted to run and hands wanted to hurt, Peanut began to look around.

HELP PEANUT BY NAMING THINGS YOU CAN SEE AROUND YOU.

Peanut looked back at Wise Owl. The feelings weren't so **BIG** anymore. They were kind of small. Peanut's mind was clear, and the **Protector Brain** had cooled down.

"What just happened?" said Peanut. "Where did the **BIG** feelings go?"

"Looking around signals your **Protector Brain** that you are safe. When it realizes there is no life-threatening danger, it cools down. Then you feel more at ease, and your Wise Mind can work to help you."

All of a sudden, Peanut noticed a tummy grumble. "Wow – I guess I'm hungry! I didn't even notice that when I was having the **BIG** feelings."

"Yes, that's because your Wise Mind was able to hear the signal from your tummy, once your **Protector Brain** quieted down. It's amazing what you can discover about your body when your Wise Mind is activated!"

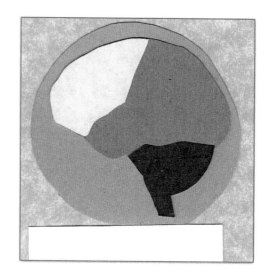

"Hey, now I know why your name is Wise Owl. It's because you know so much about **BIG** feelings, and you're really good at activating your Wise Mind!" Peanut grinned.

The next day, Peanut was kicking rocks around the backyard. Wise Owl suspected that this would be a good time for the last lesson.

"I'm so mad right now!" Peanut said. "Mamma said I couldn't have – " Wise Owl interrupted. "Where do you notice the mad feelings Peanut?" Peanut looked at Wise Owl and shrugged. "I don't know."

"You can point to where they are," suggested Wise Owl.

"Here." (It was Peanut's heart.)

"Is it hot or cold?"

"HOT!"

"Is it prickly, bubbly, or still?"

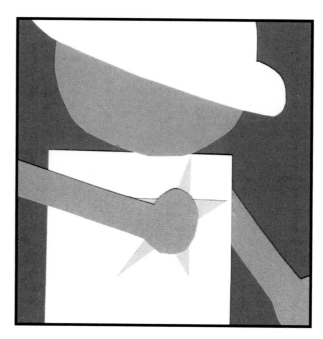

"It's prickly ALL OVER."

"Okay. Let's hang out with that hot, prickly feeling in your heart for a little bit."

Peanut blinked a few times, and then let out a big sigh.

"Now what do you notice?" asked Wise Owl. "I don't feel the hot, prickly feeling so **BIG** anymore," Peanut said. "Hey, that feels pretty good!"

"Interesting!" said Wise Owl. "Just by noticing where you felt the mad feelings, you were able to help your **Protector Brain** cool down. Let's spend a few minutes letting that good feeling sink in."

POINT TO THE PLACE IN YOUR BODY WHERE YOU NOTICE MAD FEELINGS.

"Wise Owl.... Did you ever have a really **BIG** feeling?" asked Peanut curiously.

Wise Owl smiled a soft smile, with a look of knowing inside big, round eyes.

"I still do," Wise Owl offered. "I've learned – through lots of practice – how to use my gift to help myself and help others."

"Just like you've helped me!" exclaimed Peanut. "Wise Owl, I promise to practice what you've taught me so I can help others with their **BIG** feelings too."

That night, the full moon rose high in the sky, and moonbeams drifted over the warm, soft blankets on Peanut's bed. Sweet sleep was heavy on Peanut's eyelids, and thoughts of Wise Owl's lessons danced in the air above the bed.

Peanut is a kid who still has **BIG** feelings.

Now, Peanut knows how to listen to those **BIG** feelings and help them so the **Wise Mind** can work to help solve problems.

Someday, Peanut's **BIG** feelings will help heal the world.

IMPLEMENTATION GUIDE: TEACHING WISE OWL'S LESSONS

Carefully and thoroughly read these recommendations in their entirety before using any of these interventions with a child.

1. Your body gives you important clues. (Activity: Body Map)

It's critical that you speak as little as possible and give the child free choice over every part of the body map. They will be transferring their internal state to the paper, so you will want to treat the paper with great care, as though it's their literal body.

Start by having them lie down on a long piece of paper.

Ask them what color they'd like you to use to trace the outline. Tell them where your marker is as you trace around their body (…now I'm next to your knee, and now the bottom of your foot, etc.).

Observe their face and body for any clues of discomfort (tension or rigid holding), and stop and check in if needed. Most kids find the tracing to be comfortable and even enjoyable, but if for any reason the child you're working with doesn't, ask if they would like to get up, and you can draw in the rest.

Next, it is their turn. Follow Wise Owl's script, leaving lots of space between directions for the child to create what comes up:

"Think of a time you had a really BIG feeling." (You might direct the process a little more by specifying a big, comfortable feeling or a big, uncomfortable feeling; see the section on Grounding and Safety for more on this.)

"Draw how that feeling felt on the paper. You can use any colors or materials you want and make it look however you want." (Resist directing the process further. Children often need several minutes of quiet space to find their way with this intervention.)

If the child is having trouble coming up with anything to put on the map, or has left the heart and/or gut area empty, you can offer the following guidance as needed:

"How about your heart? What was happening there?"

"And your belly? Was it hot or cold? Prickly, bubbly, or still? Light or heavy?"

Make short, direct observations while the child is drawing (you're using the red marker now...you put some green on that...). Do not state inferences or assumptions about the drawing (those are your angry feelings...that red must mean it was hot...you only drew in your brain area, don't you feel anything anywhere else?).

When the child appears finished, ask if they are finished, and say "Tell me about what you drew." Ask about any areas they leave out. Ask about temperature, texture, and weight of the different areas. When they have finished telling the story of their body map ask them what they would like to do with it. Most children want to hang their body map in their bedroom. Help them find a location where siblings and pets will not disturb it.

2. Your Wise Mind doesn't work very well while you're having BIG feelings because the Protector Brain takes all your brain power. (Activity: Brain Model)

For this lesson, you will need a basic diagram of the brain which shows a side view. 3D models are great because children can touch them and turn them in their hands. On the model, point to the lower brain regions (cerebellum, brain stem, and limbic area) and tell the child, "This is the Protector Brain." Next, point to the frontal lobes and say, "This is the Wise Mind." Hand the model to the child, and ask them to show you the Protector Brain and Wise Mind.

Next, hold up your hand, palm flat and facing away from you. Invite the child to do the same. Fold your thumb in. Your forearm and thumb represent the spinal cord, brain stem, and limbic areas. Tell the child "This is your Protector Brain," and point to the corresponding area on your hand and arm. Next, fold your fingers over your thumb. This represents the cortex. Point to it, and tell the child "This is your Wise Mind." (The prefrontal cortex is the specific area being referred to as "Wise Mind," but for this it is best to simplify and generalize all of the fingers over the thumb, the cortex, as the Wise Mind.)

Use this explanation with the child; adapting to their developmental stage:

"Our bodies send all kinds of signals up to our brains. When something is uncomfortable, it sends a signal up to the brain that may get translated as danger. When this happens, it causes our lid to flip (lift your fingers off of your thumb), and we can no longer think to solve our problems. We can help the lid come back down and get the Wise Mind working by helping the body focus on a comfortable feeling. When the Protector Brain feels safe, the lid comes back on and we can think to solve the problem that caused the lid to flip."

3. You can help your Wise Mind work by noticing what's around you. (Activity: Noticing)

The Protector Brain evolved to be aware of our surroundings. This makes sense when you consider our ancestors, who could be eaten if they didn't pay attention to the environment around them. We can use this tool to our advantage today, when we sense that our Protector Brain has been triggered by strong signals in our bodies. Moving the head and eyes from side to side and up and down creates a reward feedback loop which quiets the alerted lower brain systems.

Here's a way you can use this intervention with a child: When you notice the child feeling mildly uncomfortable - maybe they're feeling anxious about talking about their feelings with you, or perhaps you engage them in a game and get a big lead on them and they start to feel angry or sad - reflect what you observe.

A note on observations (this is important); You are only reflecting back to the child what you can see, as a mirror. This might sound like, "I can see your eyes looking down and your eyebrows are furrowed, like this (demonstrate)," or, "I notice you are shifting side to side in your chair." Observations are different than evaluations, where you are drawing conclusions about what you observe. An evaluation might sound like, "You are feeling angry because you're losing the game," or, "You get nervous when I talk about feelings." Resist the temptation to interpret what you observe.

After reflecting your observation to the child, invite them to let their eyes move around the room. You give them as much time as they would like, and join them as a way of demonstrating what you are asking them to do. After at least a couple of minutes have passed, return a soft gaze toward the child, and when their eyes settle on you, ask if they are complete. Next, ask them to share what they notice about their body. If they have a hard time finding anything, you can share more observations about changes you saw. Look at their heartbeat, breathing, and energy level as starting places.

Give a concluding statement. "Hmm…interesting! Just by allowing your eyes to move around the room, you were able to xyz (slow your breathing, calm your body, feel more comfortable, etc)." Keep it short and simple. If the child seems interested, you can briefly explain the science of it by saying "Looking around makes you aware of your surroundings. Being aware of your surroundings tells your Protector Brain you are safe."

Once the child understands that this tool can help them, they are more likely to respond positively in the moment when their lid is flipped. This tool works well with younger kids, even though they might not understand it's helpful. They will naturally respond to being guided by a trusted caregiver.

This is not distraction. You are not asking the brain to engage in a thought process about anything in the room. You are merely using the turning head and side-to-side eye movements as a mechanism to soothe the lower brain systems.

4. You can help your Wise Mind work by paying attention to the clues your body gives you. (Activity: Sensation Awareness)

Counter to popular thought, the brain initiates a fairly small portion of the signals down to the body. The majority of information flow between the brain and the body actually comes from the sensory information of the body into the brain. Many people are unaware of this information available to them, and are, therefore, unaware of how those signals impact the state of their mind. Promoting awareness of this information from the body integrates the neural connections between the lower brain regions (referred to in this book as the Protector Brain; the brain stem and limbic regions) and higher centers (referred to as the Wise Mind; the prefrontal cortex).

When we learn to become aware of how a particular sensation impacts our thought processes, we can use our Wise Minds to help us feel better. For example, many kids can identify uncomfortable sensations in their belly and label that "anxiety." We typically train children to look for a logical reason for this discomfort, which takes them into their heads and away from what is really happening within. This also teaches them that something outside of them is causing them to feel this way, and the only way to feel better is to change whatever that is. When we bring the focus instead to their somatic experience, we bring the locus of control back within and empower them to feel better without depending on the people or situations around them to change.

This intervention requires being with the child during a time when an intense emotional state is starting to emerge. It also requires that a relationship of trust and mutual respect has been established between the child and adult. The adult must be attuned to the internal state of the child and the micro-nonverbal movements that indicate an emotion is coming up. Examples of this include the child becoming suddenly quiet or agitated, change in facial expression, change in position of their body in relationship to the adult, and other directly observable behavior.

Follow the script from Wise Owl, allowing plenty of time for the child to formulate a response. Interrupt any logical thought process about the emotional state (Example: In the book, Peanut is upset at Mamma. Instead of engaging in problem solving about the situation, Wise Owl directs Peanut to focus on the sensations being experienced.)

"Where do you notice your feelings? You can point to where the feelings are. Is it hot or cold? Prickly, bubbly, or still? Okay. Let's hang out with that {describe sensation} feeling in your {location in their body} for a little bit. Now what do you notice?"

Help the child track the intensity of the sensation. It may increase, and the child can stop anytime they would like. Direct them to notice their surroundings if they want to take a break. The adult's job is to provide a calm base and send the message that the child is completely safe, despite the information from the body that the brain is interpreting as alarm.

From here, the adult invites the child to explore the edges of their sensations, and in this way, the child is able to increase their capacity to be with the sensation as it moves through.

Highlight any findings the child comes to. Allow time for this new awareness to really sink in by directing the child to stay with any feelings of comfort that have arisen.

During a BIG feeling, don't underestimate the comforting power of a nurturing, supportive touch and quiet, gentle presence. No learning can happen during a BIG feeling, so all interventions should be aimed at safety, then soothing.

Grounding and Safety

You're likely reading this book to help a child with uncomfortable BIG feelings. Children first need a grounding base of comfortable and safe sensations they can draw from. Focus on building awareness and connection to safety and comfort in the lessons first, before really getting into the uncomfortable sensations associated with anger, fear, and anxiety. Another way to do this is through yoga or any movement/posture.

Integrating Yoga to Create Grounding and Safety

No expertise is required to use yoga in your safety-building approach. You do need to have some experience with yoga before starting, so you know what to expect with each pose to prevent injuries (for example, in warrior pose, you want to be sure the front knee doesn't extend past the toes). You can use a few basic poses, such as tree, warrior, child, and mountain.

Invite the child to form a pose with you. Encourage them to move slowly and find their balance, breaking the pose down into micro-steps and entering into it one step at a time.

As the child moves with the pose, ask them what they are noticing. If they are unable to answer, ask if they can point to a place where they are feeling this pose. What is there? You can talk about where you are feeling the pose to inquire whether the child also notices sensation there. Validate whatever the child finds by saying, "Ah, yes! You feel strong in your leg muscles."

Make the connection to safety and grounding by asking whether the sensation is comfortable, uncomfortable, or neutral. Ask how it is to feel this comfortable or neutral sensation, and direct them to stay with the sensation as long as they would like. If they feel an uncomfortable sensation, validate that also and be curious about how they could shift the pose slightly to create more comfort. This exercise is all about finding comfort, so use your curiosity to help the child find it and then stay with it long enough to sink in.

You can bring this memory back to the child later on to help shift their focus away from something overwhelming/uncomfortable to a place of safety within.

Prevention vs. Intervention

The more these tools and ideas are explored in times when the child is open to learning, the more useful they will be when the Protector Brain is activated. The noticing tool can be used without prior experience, however, by simply inviting the child to notice specific things in their environment that require them to turn their head to see. You can practice noticing sensations any time, with or without the specific lessons offered in this book. This will help build those neural connections casually, in everyday experiences, without the "pressure" of performance or right/wrong ideas.

A Note on Touch

We have forgotten the value of nurturing touch. Increase positive (skin-to-skin when possible) touch for children who experience overwhelm by intense emotional states. This contact helps to balance the nervous system and increase its ability to "process" incoming sensory inputs that can contribute to overwhelm and disregulation.

Using the Tools: When & How Much

Be sensitive to each child's individual needs and stop if they are not open to learning.

Closing Thoughts

This book was created to provide an accessible way for all adults and children to learn tools for managing intense emotional states. Please do not hesitate to seek further guidance from qualified mental health practitioners if you find these suggestions do not improve your child's ability to regulate, or if you'd like some support with implementation. The tools and information contained in this book are inspired in part by the profound, groundbreaking works of Peter Levine and Dan Siegel and by the wisdom of many children.

May this book be a blessing to each person who finds it in their hands.

Jenifer Trivelli

thank you

Stephanie Matlock Allen, Wise Editor

Sharon Roemmel, Creative Encourager

Eric Jensen, my Constant

Made in the USA
Columbia, SC
16 April 2023

14981255R00020